P9-CRZ-378

For Beth Ertel—Happy Birthday!
Big huge hugs and kisses!
—L. F.

For Cole and Miranda

—B. P.

Heart to Heart with mallory

by Laurie Friedman
illustrations by Barbara Pollak

darbycreek

MINNEAPOLIS

CONTENTS

A WORD FROM MALLORY

This morning, I found two strange things in the mailbox. One was an invitation. The other was a package.

First, let me tell you about the invitation. It was addressed to my whole family, and it was from my next door neighbor, Mr. Winston. He invited Mom and Dad and Max and me to a Valentine's Party. And the invitation said: Dress Fancy.

Now, you're probably thinking that's nice because parties are lots of fun. But trust me when I tell you it's strange too, because ever since I moved to Wish Pond Road, I've never known Mr. Winston to throw a party.

Even Joey, my on-the-street best friend,

would tell you that his dad isn't exactly the party-throwing type.

Strange, huh? But wait till you hear about the package. It's even stranger.

My grandma sent me a diary, and she sent it with a note that said: Dear Honey Bee, You can tell your deepest thoughts and feelings to your diary. Love, Grandma.

When I read the note, I called Grandma and reminded her that I didn't need to tell my deepest thoughts and feelings to a diary because I have a best friend for that.

But Grandma said there might be some things I can't tell Mary Ann. And she said it in an I-know-things-that-you-don't sort of way.

All of a sudden, Mr. Winston is throwing a fancy party, and Grandma thinks there are things I can't tell my best friend. Think what you want, but I think things are getting a little strange around here.

And I'm not sure I like it.

KEEP OUT!

This is the

Top-Secret

Diary

of Mallory

McDonald

TOP SECRET

9

Winston
Wish Pond Rd

The McDonalds
17 Wish Pond Road

AN iNViTaTion

❋ The favour of a reply is requested by February 10

M _____

○ will attend
○ cannot attend

total number of people _____

MY LOVE   MARRY US

An Invitation

SATURDAY MORNING, AT MY DESK

Dear Diary,

I haven't even started writing in you and it already feels weird.

Whenever I write "Dear" anything, it's always Dear Mary Ann. But since Grandma gave you to me as a gift, I feel like I have to fill up these pages. I hope I don't hurt your feelings if I tell you that's not something I really want to do.

But the thing is, I have something to tell you. Actually, I have something to show you, and that something is an invitation. It's from Mr. Winston. He's having a Valentine's Party. Wait till you see the invitation! Mr. Winston wrote a mushy poem about LOVE!

If you ask me, it's very "un" Mr. Winston, but I don't care. I love parties (especially the kind where you get to dress up) and I can't wait to go to this one.

♡ *Mallory*

P.S. I can't decide if I should wear my pink skirt with the ruffly top or my red dress with hearts on it.

Ruffles?   <u>OR</u>   Hearts?

P.P.S. The good news: I have three weeks to decide because that's when the party is. The bad news: I have to wait three weeks for the party to get here. (Boo Hoo! I hate to wait!)

Love is...

Love is like a flower, beautiful and rare.

Love is a special feeling, none other can compare.

Love is a magician, cloaked in mystery.

Love can help illuminate things we can not see.

Love is a fuzzy sweater; it warms us deep inside.

Love is all around us; it leaves no place to hide.

Love is a precious gift; simple, clear and true.

Love is at its best when it reaches out for you.

By Frank Winston

Please join me for a celebration of love.

Date: Valentine's Day

Place: The Winston House,
             15 Wish Pond Road

Time: 7 p.m.

R.S.V.P.   Frank, Winnie, Joey,
             or Grandpa Winston

Dress: Fancy!

SATURDAY AFTERNOON, AT MY DESK

Dear Diary,

Don't you just love, love, LOVE that invitation? I can't wait to tell Mary Ann about the party!

♡ *Mallory*

SATURDAY AFTERNOON, BACK AT MY DESK

Dear Diary,

Guess what? I don't have to tell Mary Ann about the party. She already knows about it because she's invited too!

Listen to this. After lunch, I was skateboarding with Joey when he said to me, "Hey, did you know Mary Ann is coming to visit in three weeks?"

So I said, "Mary Ann's not coming to

visit in three weeks. I'm her best friend. Don't you think I would know if she was?"

But Joey kept on skateboarding and when he was about to jump a rock, he said, "She is coming. And so is her mom. They're coming for the valentine's party that my dad is throwing."

When Joey said that, I stopped skateboarding. I put my foot on the rock that Joey was about to jump so he had to stop too. "Really?" I said to him like "Is

TELL ME WHAT YOU KNOW!

that really true and can you tell me more?"

And Joey did.

"I heard my dad on the phone with Mary Ann's mom this morning," he said. "He asked her if she'd found a dress for the party yet. Then he said he can't wait to see what she's going to wear."

That's when Joey went back to skateboarding. But not me. How could I keep skateboarding when my mind was busy filling up with questions like:

Why would Mr. Winston be talking on the phone to Mary Ann's mom?

Why would he invite Mary Ann and her mom to his party?

And why would he care what Mary Ann's mom is wearing to the party?

So I asked Joey another question that was on my mind. "Hey Joey, I know your dad and Mary Ann's mom have been out on a few dates, but do they talk on the phone a lot?"

Joey stopped skateboarding and looked at me. "Define a lot," he said.

"Talking on the phone to someone every day is a lot," I said to Joey.

And when I said that, Joey laughed. He said he thinks his dad talks to Mary Ann's mom at least ten times a day. He said that every time he walks into his house, that's what his dad is doing.

Now I know what I need to be doing, and that is getting some answers. I want to know why Mr. Winston is spending all his time on the phone with Mary Ann's mom.

♡ Mallory

SATURDAY NIGHT, ON THE COUCH WITH MY FAVORITE BABYSITTER

Dear Diary,

I began my search for answers tonight. I started with my babysitter, Crystal.

She says she's good at knowing things about people. Sometimes when she babysits, she brings a little crystal ball with her. She says when she looks into it, she gets the answers she's looking for.

So tonight, I asked her if she would please look into her crystal ball and get an answer for me. I asked her if she could tell me what's going on between Joey's dad and Mary Ann's mom.

Crystal looked into her crystal ball. Then she said she needed more information.

So I gave her some.

"It's like this," I explained to her. "First, Mary Ann's mom came here to visit, and she went out on a date with Joey's dad. They had a good time, so they went out on more dates. Now, Joey's father, who never throws parties, is throwing a fancy Valentine's party, and he invited Mary Ann and her mom. And he's spending all of his time talking on the phone to her."

When I finished giving Crystal this information, I told her to look into her crystal ball and give me my answer.

But she said she didn't need a crystal ball to answer this question. "It sounds to me like they're in love," she said.

"Please look into your ball and make sure you're right," I said to Crystal.

So she looked, then she nodded her head like she was sure she knew what she was talking about.

But there's only one thing I'm sure about . . . and that's that Crystal needs a new crystal ball.

♡ *Mallory*

BAD BALL

SUNDAY MORNING, AT THE BREAKFAST TABLE WITH MOM AND DAD AND MAX AND A BOX OF CHOCOLATE DOUGHNUT HOLES

Dear Diary,

This morning, while Max was eating chocolate doughnut holes and Mom and Dad were reading the newspaper, I walked into the kitchen.

"Mallory, would you like a doughnut

hole?" Dad asked me.

But I told him I didn't want a doughnut hole. What I wanted was an answer. "Mom, Dad," I asked. "Are Mary Ann's mom and Joey's dad in love?"

When I asked that, Mom put down her coffee cup and gave Dad a look. Dad gave her a look back. "They enjoy each other's company," Mom said.

That didn't sound like much of an answer to me. "Does that mean they're in love?" I asked.

"It means they'd like to spend more time together," said Dad.

That didn't sound like an answer either.

So I asked my question again. A little louder. "CAN SOMEBODY PLEASE TELL ME, AND TELL ME NOW, IF MARY ANN'S MOM AND JOEY'S DAD ARE IN LOVE?"

And when I asked it like that, I got an answer. "Yes, Mallory," said Mom. "Mary Ann's mom and Joey's dad are in love."

And even though Mom answered my question, it made me have a whole lot more.

Like how can they be in love if they live in different cities? And why would they be in love anyway? And are they planning to go off and get married and live happily ever after just like people do on TV?

When I asked those questions, Mom and Dad smiled at each other. But I guess I didn't look like I was in the mood for

them to smile, because Dad stopped smiling and started explaining.

He told me that it would be more convenient if they lived in the same place, but that all it means is that they will have to work a little harder at planning to see each other.

Then he said it's always difficult to explain why two people love each other, but that Joey's dad and Mary Ann's mom have a lot in common and enjoy being together.

Then Dad told me that he didn't know if they would get married, that we'd all have to just wait and see.

There's just one problem: I'm scared if I wait I won't like what I'm going to see.

♡ Mallory

SUNDAY NIGHT, SITTING AT MY DESK WITH CHEESEBURGER

Dear Diary,

I keep thinking about my conversation this morning with Mom and Dad. I know I'm not the wait-and-see type.

I know something else too.

I know what Grandma meant when she said there might be some things I can't tell Mary Ann. She thinks I can't tell Mary Ann that it's NOT a good idea for her mom and Joey's dad to be in love.

But Grandma is wrong about that. I CAN tell Mary Ann and I KNOW she will agree. Mary Ann and I agree on just about everything.

I'm going to call Mary Ann right now and get this whole thing straightened out.

♡ *Mallory*

See! We agree on <u>everything</u>!

<u>SUNDAY NIGHT, 6:36,</u>
<u>AT THE PHONE IN THE KITCHEN</u>

Dear Diary,

I just tried to call Mary Ann. Her line is busy.

♡ Mallory

SUNDAY NIGHT, 6:52, STILL AT THE PHONE IN THE KITCHEN

Dear Diary,

I just tried again.

Her line is still busy.

♡ *Mallory*

beep!
beep!
beep!

7:11

STILL BUSY! I wonder who is on the phone at Mary Ann's house.

♡ *Mallory*

7:48

Dear Diary,

I just got back from Joey's house. I went over there to return a comic book I borrowed from Joey.

But that's not why I really went.

I wanted to see what the Winstons were doing. Here's what I found out: Joey and Winnie were doing their homework, Grandpa Winston was reading a book, and guess what Mr. Winston was doing? HE WAS ON THE PHONE!
♡ *Mallory*

7:53
Dear Diary,
I just called Mary Ann again. Her line is still busy. I think I know who is on the phone.
♡ *Mallory*

8:11
Still busy.

8:22

Still busy.

8:29

Dear Diary,

I bet you think I'm going to write "Still busy." But you're wrong. I don't know if Mary Ann's phone is still busy because Mom won't let me call again to find out. She says I have to go to bed.

♡ *Mallory*

SUNDAY NIGHT, IN MY BED WITH CHEESEBURGER

Dear Diary,

With all due respect (I have always wanted to use these words even though they don't make much sense), I can't fall asleep.

I wish I could have talked to Mary Ann tonight. But the first thing I'm going to do when I get home from school tomorrow is call her.

I don't like this whole Mary Ann's-mom-talking-all-night-on-the-phone-with-Joey's-dad thing. It's keeping me from sleeping.

♡ *Mallory*

P.S. Writing in a journal in the dark while you're holding a flashlight is not easy to do, but this is the last time I will have to do it because after I call Mary Ann tomorrow and straighten this whole thing out, I won't have anymore sleepless nights.

fun!

10

SPEE
LIMIT
25

a t r i p

tra

*

atlas
the road
& TRAVEL GUIDE

MAP

↑

clic

*

bon voyage!

beep
beep

adventu

a Trip

MONDAY AFTER SCHOOL, AT THE DESK IN THE KITCHEN

Dear Diary,

We hardly know each other, but I'm going to tell you something private.

I have an EMERGENCY! (Not a medical emergency, a Mallory emergency!)

Someone is going on a trip and that someone is not me.

Here's how I found out:

Right when I got home from school, I called Mary Ann. I told her I had something BIG to tell her. I was going to tell her how I thought it was a bad idea about her mom and Joey's dad being in love, and how I knew she would think so too.

But before we even started talking

about that, Mary Ann said she had
something HUGE to tell me. She told me
that Joey is going on a trip to visit her!

You probably think you're hearing
things, because that's what I thought when
I heard her say it. So I'll say it again.

JOEY IS GOING TO VISIT MARY ANN!!!!!!!!!!

Can you believe it? I can't!

Four days from now, Joey and his dad,
and his sister, Winnie, are going to see
Mary Ann and her mom for the
weekend. Four days from
now, they will be going to
my old neighborhood to see
my best friend.

When Mary Ann finished
telling me her huge news,
she asked me what my
big news was. But
hearing her huge news

made me not want to tell her my big news. So I told her I forgot what I was going to say. Then I hung up the phone.

♡ *Mallory*

P.S. I was so surprised when Mary Ann told me Joey and Winnie are going to visit her that I didn't even ask why they're going to visit. I'm going to go call Mary Ann back right now. I'm sure there is a very good explanation for all of this.

STILL AT THE KITCHEN DESK, 10 MINUTES LATER

Dear Diary,

The good news: there is an explanation for why the Winstons are going to visit Mary Ann.

The bad news: the explanation stinks.

Here it is: When I asked Mary Ann why Joey and Winnie and Mr. Winston would be going to visit her, she told me that they're going to visit her and her mom because her mom and Joey's dad are IN LOVE!

She said her mom said they want to spend lots more time getting to know each other and each other's families.

And that's not all she said.

She said that now that her mom is in love, she gets to have toaster waffles and chocolate milk for dinner and stay up past her bedtime.

She said the reason for that is because her mom is so busy talking on the phone to Joey's dad that she doesn't spend a lot of time cooking for her or remembering her bedtime.

But Mary Ann said she's glad because

she loves toaster waffles and hates going to bed. Then, Mary Ann said one more thing. She said now that her mom and Joey's dad are in love, she gets to call Mr. Winston by his first name, Frank.

I can just hear her:

Frank, isn't it a beautiful day?

Frank, would you like to see me ride my bike?

Frank, can you please pass the meatballs?

I can't believe she gets to do this! I have known "Frank" much longer than she has, and I still have to call him Mr. Winston.

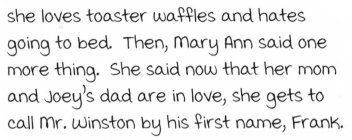 *Mallory*

P.S. In case you're wondering how my I-don't-think-it's-a-great-idea-for-your-mom-and-Joey's-dad-to-be-in-

love-and-I-know-you'll-agree-because-we-agree-on-everything talk went with Mary Ann . . . DON'T!

Grandma was right. There are some things I can't tell Mary Ann.

MONDAY NIGHT, IN MY BED (JUST BACK FROM MOM AND DAD'S BED)

Dear Diary,

I couldn't sleep. I tried counting sheep and cats and dogs and pigs. I even tried singing myself to sleep, but Max came into my room and told me that if I said one more word I'd be sleeping outside (and he didn't say it very nicely).

When he said that, I scooped up Cheeseburger and went upstairs to Mom and Dad's room and told them I would have to sleep with them tonight.

But they said I had to sleep in my own room. So I told them what I've been thinking ever since this afternoon.

I told them they haven't been very good parents lately.

When I said that, they acted shocked

and surprised. They said, "Mallory, can you please tell us what in the world you're talking about?"

So I did. "Mom, Dad, why didn't you tell me about the Winstons' trip to see Mary Ann and her mom?"

"Mallory," said Mom, "I just found out about the trip today."

"So why didn't you tell me when you found out?" I asked.

Then Mom and Dad started talking at the same time:

I WAS GOING TO TELL YOU, BUT MARY ANN TOLD YOU FIRST.

MALLORY, YOU ARE OVERREACTING!

So I told Mom and Dad that I wasn't overreacting. Then I told them about an expression that Mrs. Daily taught us at school. It's called "keeping people in the loop" and it means telling them what's going on.

I told them I wanted them to keep me in the loop, especially when it comes to Frank and Colleen.

Mom and Dad said they would be happy to keep me in the loop and that anytime I have a question I should feel free to ask them.

So I said I had another one.

"How come Mary Ann gets to call Mr. Winston Frank, and I have to call him Mr. Winston?" I asked Mom and Dad.

They said this was a very good question and that they didn't have an answer for it.

I asked if they could please get me one soon.
   ♡ Mallory

TUESDAY, AFTER SCHOOL

Dear Diary,

It's official. I now call Mr. Winston Frank. Just like Mary Ann.

I'm going next door. To say "hi" to Frank.
   ♡ Mallory

TUESDAY AFTERNOON, BACK FROM FRANK'S HOUSE

Dear Diary,

I didn't get to say "hi" to Frank. He was on the phone.

WHO IS FRANK TALKING TO?

But I did talk to Joey and Winnie, and I learned three new things.

New thing #1: Joey and Winnie don't have to go to school on Friday, because they're leaving early that morning to go see Mary Ann and her mom.

New thing #2: They are doing a lot of fun things this weekend. Friday night, they're going out for pizza and to see a movie. Saturday, they're going rollerblading. And Saturday night, they're going to an amusement park.

New thing #3: Joey and Winnie are going to call Mary Ann's mom Colleen.

In case you're wondering why they're going to call her Colleen, it's because Colleen is her first name.

♡ *Mallory*

P.S. Winnie told me she gets to buy a new sweater and jeans just for next weekend. She said her dad understood when she told him she wants to look extra special because it's going to be an extra-special weekend. If you ask me, she made up an "extra-special" excuse just to get new clothes.

TUESDAY NIGHT, IN MY BED

Dear Diary,

The only things I can think about are Joey and Winnie and Mary Ann at the amusement park. I think about them on the ferris wheel and the roller coaster. I think about them eating cotton candy and popcorn. I think about them laughing and talking and having a good time.

Diary, I do not like thinking about these things.

♡ *Mallory*

P.S. Do you think it's mean of me to think about Winnie getting cotton candy on her new sweater?

Oh no! My new sweater!

WEDNESDAY AFTER SCHOOL,
AT THE WISH POND

Dear Diary,

Today at school, all Joey talked about was his trip.

After school, all Max talked about was how lucky I am to be getting rid of Joey for a weekend. How come I don't feel lucky?

♡ *Mallory*

"We're Having Fun!"

NOT ME!

WEDNESDAY NIGHT, IN MY BED

Dear Diary,

Tonight at dinner, while Mom and Dad and Max were eating Moo Shue Chicken, I made a decision. I'm going to ask Frank if I can go with them this weekend to visit Mary Ann and her mom.

There's another expression that Mrs. Daily taught us at school. It's called "the more the merrier" and it means the more people that you have to do something, the more fun things will be. I am going to tell Frank that the more people that go on this trip, the more fun it will be.

I think Mrs. Daily will be very proud of me when she sees how I am using what she has taught us.

Mallory

P.S. I know Frank will say "yes." What else could he say?

THURSDAY MORNING
BEFORE SCHOOL

Mom says I can't ask Frank if I can go on the trip.

THURSDAY AFTERNOON
AFTER SCHOOL

Mom is mad at me.

I asked Frank if I can go on the trip.

Mom says she told me not to ask, but I told her I forgot.

Then Mom said she didn't believe I forgot and that starting Friday after school, I am going to be spending some

MAD MOM!

time in my room.

I guess I couldn't have gone on the trip anyway.

♥ *Mallory*

FRIDAY AFTER SCHOOL, IN MY ROOM

Dear Diary,

Joey was not in school today. The Winstons' car is not in their driveway.

Wish Pond Road is very, very, very quiet.

The only sound I hear is Cheeseburger snoring.

♥ *Mallory*

SATURDAY MORNING, BACK FROM THE WINSTONS'

Dear Diary,

When I woke up, I do what I do every Saturday morning. I got dressed, ate breakfast, and went over to Joey's house.

You're probably wondering why I would do that since Joey's not even there. But the person I wanted to talk to this morning was not Joey. It was Grandpa Winston. I wanted to find out if Joey and Winnie are having a LOT of fun or just a little bit of fun with Mary Ann.

Here's what I found out: Grandpa Winston had no idea!

He said he had no idea because no one has called him to tell him how the trip is going. He said it's a good sign that everyone is having so much fun that they

haven't had time to call home. Personally,
I don't think it's a good sign at all.
♡ *Mallory*

SATURDAY AFTERNOON, ALONE

Dear Diary,

There is no one to play with. Max said
he doesn't want to skateboard with me.
Grandpa Winston said he doesn't know
how.

SUNDAY AFTERNOON, 2:19, LOOKING OUT MY WINDOW

Dear Diary,

I'm waiting for Joey and Winnie and Frank to get home.

Dad said they should be home sometime this afternoon.

I'm going to wait right here until I see their car in their driveway. When I do, I'm going to go next door and see if they had a good time with Mary Ann.

♡ Mallory

2:38

Still no car in the Winstons' driveway.

3:18

Still no car. I'm going to take a bathroom break.

B.R.B. (Be right back.)

4:48

Dear Diary,

I took a bathroom break. I took a washing-my-hands break. I took a feeding-Cheeseburger break. I took an eating-leftover-doughnut-holes break. I even took a watching-a-baseball-game-that-I-didn't-want-to-watch-with-Dad-and-Max break.

STILL NO CAR IN THE WINSTONS' DRIVEWAY!

♡ Mallory

<u>5:11</u>

Dear Diary,

Guess what? NO CAR! I'm sick of
waiting. I have more important things to
do. I'm going to go rearrange my hair
thingies drawer.

💙 *Mallory*

<u>6:59</u>

Dear Diary,

Since I finished dinner, four things
have happened:

1. I opened my curtains and looked out
my window, and right when I did, I saw
the Winstons' car pulling into their
driveway.

2. I watched Winnie and Joey
unloading their car and they each had
something: A stuffed bear (like the kind

you win at an amusement park).

3. I closed my curtains so they couldn't see me looking at them.

4. I made a decision. I'm not going to ask Joey if he had a fun weekend. I mean, it really doesn't matter to me one way or the other if he had a fun weekend. I'm DEFINITELY not going to ask him. I don't even care if he did.

♡ *Mallory*

FOR A GREAT WEEKEND, GO TO AN AMUSEMENT PARK AND LEAVE YOUR BEST FRIEND AT HOME.

A Secret

Dear Diary,

I know a secret. I bet you want to know what it is. It's a long story, but I'll tell you.

It started this morning when I didn't walk to school with Joey like I always do. I didn't walk with him because I didn't want to hear about his weekend with Mary Ann.

But for some reason, right when I got to school, the first thing I asked Joey was if he had a fun weekend with Mary Ann.

Really, I didn't ask him. My mouth did. It just sort of started talking before I could stop it and here's what it said:

Mallory: So, how was your weekend
    with Mary Ann?
Joey: Fun.
Mallory: What did you do?
Joey: We went for pizza, rollerblading,
    and to an amusement park.
Mallory: Is that all?
Joey: Yep.
Mallory: You're not leaving anything
    out?
Joey: Nope.

And that made me wonder. I mean,
how could Joey not be leaving something
out? He was there for a whole weekend.
So I asked what I really wanted to know.
I asked him what it was like hanging out
with Mary Ann and her mom.
    And Joey said, "OK, I guess."
    Then Joey said something that

surprised me. He said he wanted to do his math.

The weird thing about that is that Joey never wants to do his math. So I did some math of my own. "YEP" and "NOPE" and "OK, I guess" just didn't add up.

"YEP" + "NOPE" + "OK, I guess" = A phone call to Mary Ann

Something told me that there was something Joey did NOT want to tell me and I knew that if I wanted to find out, I was going to have to ask someone else.

♡ *Mallory*

P.S. If you're still wondering what the secret is, stay tuned. I'm about to tell you.

MONDAY NIGHT,
ON THE FLOOR OF THE BATHROOM
I SHARE WITH MAX

Dear Diary,

I had to lock myself in the bathroom so no one can see what I'm writing.

What I'm writing is V.I.S. That's short for Very Important Stuff, and Mary Ann told me lots of it.

When I called Mary Ann to see how the weekend was with the Winstons, she told me she had one great thing, one not-so-great thing, and one big secret to tell me.

Even though I couldn't wait to hear the big secret, I was kind of scared to. So I asked Mary Ann to start with the not-so-great thing. She told me that Joey and his dad were really nice, but that Winnie barely spoke to her all weekend.

I told Mary Ann that Winnie barely

speaks to anybody and when she does, whatever she says isn't nice at all.

Then, Mary Ann told me the great thing, and you won't believe what she told me.

She told me that her mom and Joey's dad aren't just in love, they are head-over-heels in love.

I knew what she meant when she said that because Mrs. Daily taught us the expression "head-over-heels." She said that it usually refers to love and it means when two people are crazy about each other.

So I asked Mary Ann how she knew that her mom and Joey's dad are head-over-heels for each other. Mary Ann said she knows because her mom calls Frank, "my Frank" and Frank calls her mom, "my Colleen."

When Mary Ann told me that, I told her that just because they say stuff like that doesn't mean they're head-over-heels.

Then, Mary Ann told me there's more. She said that when Frank left, she heard him tell her mom that when they're not together, he's "filled with despair," and her mom said she felt exactly the same way.

I didn't actually know what that meant, so I asked Mary Ann, who said she asked her mom the same question and her mom said that it's when you're completely sad about something.

Then Mary Ann told me that she couldn't wait any longer and that she had to tell me her big secret. She made me pinky swear not to tell anybody. (Technically, you're not anybody, so I'm telling you.)

Mary Ann said that she thinks Frank will pop the question soon and that if I didn't know what question she was talking about, it is the "Will you marry me?" question.

I knew there was something Joey wasn't telling me.

♡ *Mallory*

TUESDAY MORNING, AT MY DESK AT SCHOOL

Dear Diary,

On the way to school, I asked Joey if he knew of any questions that his dad was planning to ask Colleen.

Joey said his dad probably asks Colleen questions all the time because he always asks him questions like: Will you please do your homework? And will you please clean up your room?

I knew Joey didn't know I was talking about the will-you-marry-me question, so I asked Winnie.

When I asked her, she said she had a question to ask me.

Her question: Will you please leave me alone?

The whole way to school, I didn't ask one more question.

♡ *Mallory*

STILL AT MY DESK

Dear Diary,

Right now I'm supposed to be working on a list of all the words you can make out of the letters in Valentine's Day. Mrs. Daily said we're doing this since next Saturday is Valentine's Day and next

Friday, we're having our class Valentine's party. She says she wants us to start getting into the spirit of things.

But right now, I'm working on a different list. I'm working on a list of reasons why Frank should or should not "pop the question."

If Frank pops the question . . .

☐ YES:
1. Mary Ann and her mom will probably move here, and Mary Ann will be my next door neighbor, just like she used to be before I moved.

☑ NO:
1. Mary Ann and Joey will live in the same house.

2. Mary Ann and Joey will do everything together.

3. Mary Ann and Joey will do everything together . . . WITHOUT ME!

According to my list, it is not a good idea for Frank to pop the question.

♡ *Mallory*

TUESDAY NIGHT, 7:14, AT THE KITCHEN TABLE

Dear Diary,

I'm supposed to be doing my homework. I'm trying to think about science, but the only thing I can think about is Frank popping the question, and I've decided something: I HAVE TO STOP HIM FROM DOING IT. I have to make sure if he does, there's only one thing Colleen

will say and that thing is, "NO WAY!"
 ♡ *Mallory*

TUESDAY NIGHT, 7:22, STILL AT THE KITCHEN TABLE

Dear Diary,

Now all I have to do is think of a way. How hard can it be?

 ♡ *Mallory*

WEDNESDAY NIGHT, 8:07, BACK AT THE KITCHEN TABLE

Dear Diary,

The answer is: VERY HARD. I've been trying since last night to think of a way to get Frank to NOT pop the question, and I can't think of a way. Not one, single way. Tonight, I ate spinach at dinner.

That's what Popeye does when he wants his muscles to work. I'm hoping it makes my brain work.

♡ *Mallory*

THURSDAY NIGHT

Still no ideas. I'm never eating spinach again.

yuck!

FRIDAY NIGHT

Dear Diary,

Still no ideas for how to stop Frank from popping the question.

I'm going to do what I always do when I have to do really hard thinking. I'm going to stop writing and start rubbing the sides of my head. That always helps me think.

♡ *Mallory*

FRIDAY NIGHT, 7:54, STILL AT MY DESK

Dear Diary,

I've been rubbing my head for 14 minutes and I haven't thought of one single way to stop Frank from popping the question.

Got to go. Got to rub.

♡ *Mallory*

7:56

Still rubbing.

7:58

Still rubbing.

me trying to think of a good idea

8:01

Still rubbing.

<u>8:07</u>

Dear Diary,

I've been rubbing my head for 27 minutes. I haven't gotten any ideas. The only thing I've gotten is a sore head. I'm going to pretend like I'm at the wish pond and make a wish. I wish I will think of a way in the next 5 minutes to stop Frank from asking Colleen to marry him.

I hope my wish will come true.

♥ *Mallory*

<u>8:11</u>

Dear Diary,

You won't believe what I'm about to tell you. MY WISH CAME TRUE! I thought of a brilliant plan to stop Frank from popping the question. I bet you can't wait to know what it is. So I'll tell you.

I'm going to write don't-get-married-to-each-other poems! One for Colleen and one for Frank. Once they read my poems, there's no way they'll want to marry each other. Don't you agree that my plan is brilliant?

Got to go. Got to write.

♡ *Mallory*

P.S. I'm going to sign my poems, Anonymous. (That means I'm not going to say who they're from.) YOU HAVE TO PINKY SWEAR NOT TO TELL ANYBODY!!!

Poems

FRIDAY NIGHT, 9:02, STILL AT MY DESK

Dear Diary,

It took a while, but I finally finished my don't-get-married-to-each-other poems. I wrote Colleen's on one piece of paper, and I put it in an envelope with her name on it. I did the same thing with Frank's poem. I'm going to mail them in the morning.

I think I did a really good job. Want to see what I wrote?

♡ Mallory

A poem for Colleen

Colleen, you do not want to marry poor Frank.

    He is so poor, he might rob a bank.

Colleen, you do not want to marry dumb Frank.

    He is so dumb, his mind is a blank.

Colleen, you do not want to marry bad Frank.

    He yells at his kids.

    They call him "The Crank."

Colleen, you do not want to marry cruel Frank.

    He does not keep water inside his fish tank.

Colleen, you do not want to marry "Your Frank."

    Take my advice and you'll have me to thank.

    If you marry him, you will be making a
Big, Big, BIG mistake!

Sincerely,
Anonymous

P.S. I'm not
making any
of this up!

A poem for Frank

Frank, you do not want to marry Colleen.
    She dresses each day like it's Halloween.
Frank, you do not want to marry Colleen.
    When she blows her nose,
    her S-N-O-T is green.
Frank, you do not want to marry Colleen.
    There are rats in her kitchen.
    Her house is not clean.
Frank, you do not want to marry Colleen.
    She takes candy from babies.
    That lady is MEAN!
Frank, you do not want to marry "Your Colleen."
    If you marry that lady, you'll see what I mean.

    I'm just trying to save you from making
the **Biggest** mistake of your life.

Sincerely,
Anonymous

P.S. I'm not making
    any of this up!

SATURDAY MORNING, AT MY DESK
SEARCHING EVERYWHERE!

Dear Diary,

My poems are gone! The envelopes I left here last night with Frank and Colleen's names on them are gone!

G.2.G. Got to go find my envelopes!

♡ *Mallory*

SATURDAY MORNING,
BACK AT MY DESK

Dear Diary,

The good news: I found my envelopes.

The bad news: I found one in Mom's hands and the other one in Dad's.

When I went into the kitchen this morning, Max was standing there with a big grin on his face. "You're in HUGE trouble," he said.

So I looked at Mom and Dad, who were

sitting at the kitchen table, to see if I could figure out what I did wrong, and that's when I saw that they had my envelopes, and they were OPENED! And you won't believe what they said.

> *Mom:* Dad and I are very upset that you would write these poems.
>
> *Me:* How do you know I wrote them? They're not signed by me. If you look at them, you will see that they are by ANONYMOUS!
>
> *Max:* They're in your handwriting. I found them in your room. And if you didn't write them, how would you know they are anonymous?
>
> *Me:* Shut up!
>
> *Mom:* Mallory, you're not allowed to say shut up.
>
> *Max:* So they <u>were</u> yours.

Dad: How do you think Frank and
      Colleen would feel if they read what
      you wrote?
Me: I'm going to my room!
Mom: Yes, you are, but not until you
      hear what we have to say first.

And then Mom made me listen to a
whole long speech about how what I
wrote wasn't true and it was mean and
why you shouldn't do things like that and
how I needed to adjust my attitude and
lots more blah blah blah stuff about how
nice it is when two people fall in love.
THEN, she sent me to my room, which is
where I am now and will be for the rest
of the morning.
    ♡ Mallory

Phone Calls

Dear Diary,

Mom finally let me out of my room because I had a phone call. Usually, I ♥ LOVE ♥ phone calls. But not this one. It was from Joey, and the reason I didn't like it was because of what he said.

bzzzz

Joey: Hey Mallory, does Mary Ann like to skateboard?

Me: Why do you want to know?

Joey: You know she's coming here next weekend for the party, and Dad thought it might be fun to get a new skateboard for her if you think she'd like it.

What I said: Oh. (What I didn't say: I'd like a new skateboard too.)

Joey: You know how Dad likes doing nice things for people. He wanted to do something nice for Mary Ann.

Me: (Even though it was my turn to say something, I didn't. I was too busy thinking about what Joey said about his dad doing nice things for people. It seemed to me that he likes doing nice things for one person, Mary Ann.)

Joey: Mal, you still there? Do you think you could call Mary Ann and find out? OK? I've got to go.

Then Joey hung up. Just like that. Before I even had time to say if I would or wouldn't call Mary Ann.

Since he didn't really give me a choice, I

dialed Mary Ann's number. S-L-O-W-L-Y. When the phone started to ring, I waited for Mary Ann to answer. But her mom picked up.

Colleen: Mallory, how nice to hear your voice!

Me: May I speak to Mary Ann, please?

Colleen: Sweetie, she's in the car. We were just going out to do some shopping for next weekend. Mary Ann and I have a lot to do to get ready for the party.

What I said: Oh. (What I didn't say: I'm getting sick of people spending all their time getting ready for next weekend.)

Colleen: She'll call you when we get home, OK?

Me: I just wanted to know if she wants to try skateboarding when she's here next weekend. But she probably doesn't. So don't even ask her, OK?

Colleen: No, I'm sure she'd love to. How nice of you to ask.

Me: Actually, Frank is the one who asked. He wants to buy her a new skateboard.

Colleen: That Frank is sooooo sweet! ♪

What I said: OK, bye. (What I wanted to say: Frank is really not sooooo sweet. If he asks you to marry him, you definitely should NOT!)

Then I hung up the phone and waited for Mary Ann to call me back. I waited for two whole hours.

While I was waiting, I got another phone call. This one was from Winnie.

Me: Mary Ann?

Winnie: No, it's me, Winnie. Listen, I'm at the sporting goods store in the mall with Joey and Dad. They want to know if you talked to Mary Ann yet and if we should get her a skateboard.

Me: No.

Winnie: No, what? No, you didn't talk to her? Or no, don't get her a skateboard?

Me: Um, no, I haven't talked to her yet, so maybe you shouldn't get her a skateboard.

Winnie: Dad said if you haven't talked to her, we'll just get her the skateboard and something else too. Like a makeup kit. He said he's sure she'll like one of those things. He wants to get her something she'll like. I can't think of one reason why he should, but he says he's going to.

Then Winnie hung up and all I could do was wait for Mary Ann to call me. And all I could think about was the new skateboard and makeup kit she was getting.

She didn't call until it was almost dinner time, so I had a lot of time to think about those things. And what I was thinking was that it bothers me that the Winstons are being so nice to Mary Ann and practically ignoring me.

It's not like I don't want them to be nice to her. But it's not like anybody is trying to buy a new skateboard or a makeup kit for me. It's kind of like they've forgotten that I'm their next-door neighbor.

Just when I was thinking about how they barely even know Mary Ann, and how they're spending all of their time thinking of ways to be nice to her, Mom told me to set the table (which isn't nearly as much fun as going shopping for a new dress or going to the mall to buy a new skateboard or makeup kit). I was putting down forks and knives when the phone rang. It was Mary Ann (who was really in the mood to talk).

Me: Hello.

Mary Ann: Hey! Hey! Hey! Oh Mallory, I'm so glad it's you. I have soooo much to tell you! First of all, Mom and I just got home. We shopped all day. We both bought dresses for the party next weekend. Hers is purple and gold and it has a long skirt and a lacy top. Mine is light pink on the top and dark pink on the bottom and it has a big bow on the back. We have so much to do to get ready for the party! On Monday, we're going shoe shopping. On Tuesday, we're going present shopping for Joey and Winnie and Frank. On Wednesday, we're getting manicures. Real ones, at the salon. On Thursday, we're getting haircuts, and on Friday, I get to leave school at noon and we're driving straight to Fern Falls so I'll be there right when you get home from school. I can't wait till next weekend. I can't wait till we get to get all dressed up! We're going to have so much fun! It's going to be such a great party! And Mom told me about the skateboard, and I can't wait to try skateboarding. It's all so, so, so exciting! Don't you think so too, Mallory? Don't you think everything's going to be great, great, great?

Me: Um, yeah. Great, great, great.

Then I hung up the phone. Even though Mary Ann is my best friend, this seemed like one of those times when we don't agree on everything.

♡ *Mallory*

MONDAY MORNING, STILL IN BED

Dear Diary,

I don't want to get out of bed today.

Actually, I don't want to get out of bed for six more days.

Just six more days till Frank's party.

Just six more days till Colleen says three little letters, Y-E-S, that will change my life forever. Just six more days till my best friends become best step brother and sister, or whatever it is they become when their parents decide to get married.

I am staying in bed. Just six more days.

♡ *Mallory*

MONDAY, ON THE PLAYGROUND

Dear Diary,

This morning, Mrs. Daily reminded us that this Friday we're having our Valentine's class party since Saturday is Valentine's Day.

When she said that, Pamela leaned over to my side of the desk and said she can't wait because she loves Valentine's Day.

I know Pamela was waiting for me to say that I love Valentine's Day too. But I didn't. I used to love Valentine's Day. I don't anymore.

♡ *Mallory*

WHAT'S SO GREAT ABOUT VALENTINE'S DAY?

MONDAY, AFTER SCHOOL AT MY DESK

Dear Diary,

On the way home from school, Joey asked if I wanted to do some skateboarding. "We can practice before Mary Ann gets here," he said.

I said, "Not today."

Then he asked if I wanted to take Cheeseburger on a walk with him and his dog, Murphy.

I said, "I don't feel like it."

So, he asked me if he could come over to my house. He said we could make super-sized peanut butter and marshmallow sandwiches.

But I said, "I'm not hungry."

Then Joey said, "Mallory, you love to skateboard and walk your cat and you're always hungry. You're not acting like yourself. Is everything OK?"

And then, I didn't say anything. I just shrugged my shoulders and nodded my head yes. But the real answer is no.

I just didn't feel like telling Joey that the reason I'm not acting like myself is because in exactly six days, his father is going to propose to Mary Ann's mother.

I can't even eat my favorite sandwich!

I didn't feel like telling him that if that weren't the case, I would be acting just like myself.

♡ *Mallory*

P.S. Today at school, Mrs. Daily said that we need to make valentine's cards for everyone in our class to give out at the party. What am I going to write on Joey's card? I hope you have a SWEET year with my best friend as your new stepsister?

A Secret Admirer

TUESDAY AT SCHOOL,
IN THE SUPPLY CLOSET

Dear Diary,

You will never believe where I am. I am hiding in Mrs. Daily's supply closet.

I had to come in here so NOBODY could see what I'm writing.

You won't believe what I am about to tell you.

I HAVE A SECRET ADMIRER! I know it's hard to believe but it's true. And the reason I know it's true is because my secret admirer gave me a secret card.

I found it when I came back from lunch. It was sitting right on top of my desk and it said "To Mallory From Your Secret Admirer" right on the envelope.

So I did the only thing I could do: I grabbed it off my desk and ran into the supply closet to read it.

I'm gluing it into my journal so NOBODY will ever be able to read it.

♡ *Mallory*

P.S. It worked out nicely that I'm in the supply closet. I hope Mrs. Daily won't mind that I borrowed some of her glue.

Dearest Mallory,
I'm your secret admirer.
There's something I want to say.
I can't wait to celebrate
With you on Valentine's Day.
Hugs and Kisses!
Your Secret Admirer

OOPS

AT MY DESK,
A FEW MINUTES LATER

Dear Diary,

Sorry I ripped a page out of you when I tore out the card from my secret admirer, but I had to show it to Pamela.

I wasn't going to show it to anybody, but I showed her because I can NOT figure out who my secret admirer is and I wanted Pamela to help me.

Even though she makes better grades than I do, she couldn't figure it out either.

She said that if my secret admirer had written the card, we'd be able to look at the handwriting for clues. She said with the typing, it's kind of hard to tell.

I asked Pamela if she could check the fingerprints or something, but Pamela said she didn't know how.

I wonder who my secret admirer is.

♡ *Mallory*

P.S. I'm not showing anyone else my card. I will figure this out myself.

AFTER SCHOOL

Dear Diary,

I know I said I wasn't going to show anyone else the card from my secret admirer, but I showed Joey on the way home from school. I thought since he's a boy he might know if another boy in our class sent it.

But when I asked him, he started laughing. Then he said he didn't think another boy sent it. So I asked if he sent it.

He laughed even harder.

Then he said he didn't send it.

♡ *Mallory*

WEDNESDAY, BACK IN THE SUPPLY CLOSET

Dear Diary,

Guess what? It happened again! My secret admirer gave me something else. This time I got a little heart-shaped snow globe. I found it on my desk when I came back from lunch.

It snows pink snow and hearts when you shake it.

I LOVE it, except for one thing . . . I don't know who it's from!

I can't stand
not knowing
things!!!
Especially things
like who my
secret admirer is.
But I'm going to find
out . . . AND SOON!
♡ Mallory

WEDNESDAY NIGHT

Dear Diary,

I tried finding out who my secret admirer is.

After math, I showed my snow globe to Mrs. Daily. I asked if she saw anyone leave this for me on my desk.

She said she hadn't, but that whoever did must like me a lot.

On the way home from school, I showed it to Joey. I asked if he was absolutely, positively, 100% certain that he's not my secret admirer.

He said he's absolutely, positively, 100% certain he's NOT my secret admirer.

After dinner, I showed it to Max. Even though I didn't think he could possibly be my secret admirer, I just wanted to be sure.

I am sure.

♡ *Mallory*

THURSDAY AT SCHOOL,
IN THE BATHROOM

Dear Diary,

I still have not found out who my secret admirer is.

But there is something I did find. Another present. This time I got a little red plastic heart filled with valentine's candy.

I found it sticking out of my backpack when we came back from recess.

♡ *Mallory*

P.S. I would have glued in the little red plastic heart filled with valentine's candy, but it would have been hard to shut you, so I drew a picture instead.

CANDY

To Mallory:
Love, your ♥ ♡
Secret Admirer

P.P.S. I have to quit drawing pictures and start finding out who my secret admirer is.

THURSDAY NIGHT, AT THE DESK IN THE KITCHEN

Dear Diary,

I was sitting at the desk in the kitchen eating the candy (which was very delicious) from my secret admirer and making valentines for everyone in my class and feeling very happy (even though Max kept trying to eat my candy), when the phone rang.

It was Mary Ann, and right when I picked up I started to feel not so happy because she started telling me that she is so, so, so excited for this weekend and the party to get here. She asked me if I am so, so, so excited too. I said I was.

I wish I was.

I really wish I was.

I'm trying to be.

But I'm really not.

♡ *Mallory*

IN BED WITH CHEESEBURGER

Dear Diary,

I finished my valentines and got into bed. Ever since Mary Ann called, all I've been able to think about is this weekend. When you eat a big dinner, you go to bed with a full tummy. Tonight I'm going to bed with a full brain.

There are just so many questions in it right now. I feel like my brain is a parking lot and there are no empty spaces. I keep thinking:

What will it be like when Mary Ann is here this weekend?

Will she want to be with me or the Winstons?

What will happen if Frank proposes to Colleen?

Will that make them one big, happy family? And even though that's a lot of questions, I have one more.

Even though tomorrow is Valentine's Day, which is supposed to be happy, how can I act happy on the outside, when inside, I'm really not?

♡ *Mallory*

Valentine's Day

FRIDAY MORNING, STILL IN BED

Dear Diary,

Valentine's Day is almost here. When Mom and Dad came into my room to wake me up, they were all excited about this weekend. "Happy Day-Before-Valentine's Day!" said Mom.

But when I said that I didn't see what was so happy about it, Mom started listing all the things that she thinks I should be happy about.

"You have a party at school today. Mary Ann is coming into town tonight, tomorrow is Valentine's Day, and tomorrow night is the Winstons' party," she said.

When Mom said that, I didn't say anything back. The thing is, it's kind of hard for me to enjoy a party at school and my best friend coming into town and Valentine's Day and the Winstons' party, when all I can think about is Frank and how he's probably going to ask Mary Ann's mom to marry him, and that it's going to be a special Valentine's Day for a lot of people, but I feel like I'm not one of those people.

Then Mom said that I have to be in the kitchen in ten minutes for a special Valentine's surprise.

I wonder if the surprise is that Frank's party has been cancelled.

♡ *Mallory*

AT THE KITCHEN TABLE

Dear Diary,
The surprise was heart-shaped

pancakes. Frank's party is still on.

G.2.G.2. school.

♡ *Mallory*

Love
and
Happiness

AT MY DESK

Dear Diary,

NEWSFLASH: On the way to school, Joey asked me if I'm excited for Mary Ann to come into town. I said, "Of course, she's my best friend."

Then, you won't believe what Joey said.

He said he's excited too, and that when Mary Ann gets here, he and Mary

Ann and Winnie are writing a special song to sing at the party.

NEW PROBLEM TO THINK ABOUT: If Mary Ann's mom and Joey's dad get married, will Mary Ann still be my best friend or will she be too busy doing things like writing songs with Joey and Winnie?

Tra-la-la.
♡ Mallory

P.S. Pamela just said that she can't wait until lunch is over and it's party time. Whoopee!

AT MY DESK, AFTER LUNCH

Dear Diary,
I just got back from lunch.

I was hoping this day would improve.

I was hoping my secret admirer would magically know that I'm not feeling so great and maybe leave me a secret surprise.

My secret admirer left one thing: NOTHING.

♡ Mallory

STILL AT MY DESK

Mrs. Daily just said that as soon as we finish math, we're going to start our party.

Pamela said she can't wait to finish math. Even though it's not my favorite subject, today I don't mind doing it. I'm more in a math mood than I am in a party mood.

♡ Mallory   I ♡ MATH

<u>AT HOME, ON MY BED</u>
<u>WITH CHEESEBURGER</u>

Dear Diary,

I just got home from school. I don't have much time to write because Mom says Mary Ann and her mom should be here any minute.

I will quickly tell you about the Valentine's party at school. It will be easy to do quickly because there isn't much to tell. I wasn't in the mood for a party.

I wasn't in the mood to eat heart-shaped cookies with pink icing.

I wasn't in the mood to eat chocolate candy with red sprinkles.

I wasn't even in the mood to read my valentine's cards.

And I'm still not in the mood. My valentine's cards are shoved into my backpack, which is where I put them during the party and where they will stay for good.

I will never be in the mood to read them.

I have to go. Mom is calling me. Guess who is here?

♡ *Mallory*

FRIDAY NIGHT, IN MY BATHROOM, NO TIME TO WRITE

Dear Diary,

This is going to be a quickie because Mary Ann is here and she doesn't even know I have you. I told her I was going to the bathroom while she gets ready for the fashion show. You heard right. She's going to model the dress she's wearing to the party tomorrow night.

♡ *Mallory*

FRIDAY NIGHT, IN BED WITH A FLASHLIGHT

Dear Diary,

I have to use a flashlight to write in you because Mary Ann is asleep next to me. She went to bed early because she said she wants to wake up early to go over to Joey's so they can work on the song. It's a good thing I don't have to get up early to work on a song because I CAN'T SLEEP!

 *Mallory*

P.S. I'm pretending like I'm at the wish pond and making a wish. I wish I will get bitten by bedbugs so I won't have to go to the party tomorrow night.

BED BUGS

A Party

Dear Diary,

I have three things to tell you.

One: I was not bitten by bedbugs.

Two: I'm still going to the party tonight.

Three: Mary Ann is at Joey's. Song writing.

♡ *Mallory*

8:47

Mary Ann is still at Joey's.

9:17

Still at Joey's. Still song writing.

117

9:56

MARY ANN IS STILL AT JOEY'S!

HOW LONG CAN IT TAKE TO WRITE A
STUPID SONG?

10:18

Dear Diary,

Mary Ann is still at Joey's.

This is getting ridiculous. It is also
rude. Mary Ann is a guest at my house
and she is spending all of her time next
door.

I'm going to call her and tell her to
come home now.

I'm giving her three minutes, and then
I'm calling.

♡ Mallory

10:21

It's been three minutes.

I'm going to give her three more minutes.

Then I'm definitely calling.

10:24

Three more minutes. That's it. Just three more minutes. I mean it.

10:27

One more three more minutes. Then that's really it.

10:31

Dear Diary,

It's been four minutes. I'm going to call now, but first I'm going to see if Mom or Dad or Max needs the phone. I don't want to be rude (like some people).

♥ *Mallory*

10:32

Dear Diary,

I just called. Joey answered the phone, so I asked him how the song for tonight was coming along. You won't believe what he said.

He said it wasn't! He said they tried to make up a song to sing at the party but they couldn't come up with anything so they ended up watching TV instead.

Can you believe that?!?!

I didn't even ask Joey the question I wanted to ask him, which was, "If you were just watching TV, why didn't you call me to come watch with you?"

I didn't ask it because I already know the answer, which is: they're not even a family yet and they've already forgotten about me.

This is great. Just great.

♡ *Mallory*

SATURDAY AFTERNOON, IN THE PANTRY

Dear Diary,

I have exactly ten seconds to write in you. I have to go help Mary Ann get ready.

I have to help her zip her dress. I have to help her tie her bow. I have to help her put on her makeup.

Usually, I love helping Mary Ann. But tonight, I feel like Cinderella helping one of her stepsisters get ready for the ball.

♡ *Cinder-Mallory*

SATURDAY NIGHT, IN MY CLOSET

Dear Diary,

I can't believe I found you.

It was hard because I had to look under the piles of clothes that Mary Ann left on the floor of my closet.

♡ *Mallory*

The tale of Cinder-Mallory

STILL IN MY CLOSET

Mom would have a meltdown if she saw this mess, but I'll have to clean it up later. It's almost party time.

Hopefully the party and the BIG secret won't be too bad. I have to quit writing now . . . so I can cross my fingers.

♡ *Mallory*

IN MY BED WITH CHEESEBURGER AND A FLASHLIGHT

Dear Diary,

It's 12:47 a.m. That's after midnight in case you haven't learned to tell time yet. It also happens to be the latest I've ever stayed up.

If Mom knew I was writing in you this late, I know she'd be even madder than if she saw the mess in my closet. But I can't sleep until I tell you about the party.

Mary Ann is sound asleep next to me. And I'm really glad she is because I have a lot to tell you.

First of all, the party was really red. Frank put red roses all over his house. There were red roses in the living room. There were red roses in the dining room. There were even red roses in the bathroom!

The food was red too. Frank served chicken with a red sauce and a salad with miniature tomatoes. He had red drinks too. Red wine for the grownups and Shirley Temples for the kids. He even had a big, red cake for dessert!

AND . . . Frank wore a red shirt. I know, it's hard to imagine him doing that, but he did!

There were TONS of people at the party. Everyone who lives on our street, some people that Frank works with, Joey's aunt and her kids, and of course, Mary Ann and her mom.

There was a band too. They played a lot of love songs that Frank said were just right for Valentine's Day. I don't think they were just right for any day, but a lot of the grownups looked like they liked that kind of music.

I could tell you more about the party, but I bet what you really want to hear is what the big secret was. So I'll tell you. Drum roll, please.

Joey's dad asked Mary Ann's mom to marry him!

You're probably not that surprised. And I wasn't either. I bet you want to know how it happened, so I'll tell you.

First, Frank banged his spoon on the side of his champagne glass. He had to bang for a long time till everyone was quiet. (I thought he was going to break his glass, but he got lucky.) Then, he told everyone he had an announcement to make.

That's when, in front of everyone, Frank got down on his knees and took Colleen's hand in his, and he said a bunch of lovey dovey stuff to her about

...nderful she is and how much he
... ...er, and then he said, "Colleen, will
you marry me?"

And that made her start crying.

I thought she was crying because she didn't want to marry a guy who was losing his hair, and she felt a little funny telling him that after all the nice things he said about her.

But surprise, surprise. She started saying all kinds of nice stuff back about how special and kind he is and then she said, "Yes, my Frank, I will marry you." And she started crying even harder.

I asked Mom why Colleen was being such a crybaby at a party. Mom just hugged me and said they were happy tears. And when I looked at Mom, she had some tears too, which she said were also the happy kind.

And when I looked around the room, they weren't the only people with happy tears in their eyes. Mr. Winston had some too.

Everybody looked happy. Joey looked happy. Grandpa Winston looked happy. Winnie, who almost never looks happy, looked sort of happy. And Mary Ann, who was jumping around and hugging everybody and screaming, "My mom's getting married!" looked particularly happy.

The only person who didn't look happy was Max, who said he can't believe he might have to live next door to Mary Ann (except he didn't call her Mary Ann, he called her Birdbrain, which is his favorite nickname for her) again. But when Frank brought out the big, red cake and said the party was just getting started, Max started smiling again.

While Frank and Colleen were passing around cake, everybody was talking and hugging and even though I felt kind of scared about what things would be like when the Winstons and Mary Ann and her mom become one family, I also felt a little happy. I don't exactly know why, except that everybody looked so happy, it just kind of made me happy too.

♡ *Mallory*

P.S. Even though I felt a little happy, I did not start crying. I didn't want to get tears in my cake.

P.P.S. I have 2 more things 2 tell you, but not 2night. I am way 2 tired!!!!!!!!!!!!

A Heart-to-Heart

SUNDAY MORNING, AT THE WISH POND WITH CHEESEBURGER

Dear Diary,

I came out to the wish pond to write this because Mary Ann is still asleep and I didn't want to wake her up. Remember I told you that I had 2 more things to tell you?

Well, here's thing #1:

Last night, I had my first heart-to-heart.

Do you know what a heart-to-heart is? If you don't, don't feel too bad. I didn't either until last night when Joey said he wanted to have one.

It happened at the party while Frank and Colleen were passing out the cake.

Joey asked me if I would take my piece to his room. He said he had something he wanted to talk to me about. So we went to his room and sat on his bed.

I started eating cake and Joey started talking.

First, he explained to me what a heart-to-heart is.

"A heart-to-heart is a talk you have with someone when they tell you what is going on in their heart and then you tell them what is going on in yours," he said. Then he told me he used to have these kinds of talks with his mom before she died.

I told Joey that that made me feel sad thinking about the talks he used to have with his mom, but he told me not to be too sad because the talk he wanted to have with me was a happy talk.

So I told him to go ahead and tell me what was on his mind.

"You haven't exactly been yourself since this whole thing with my dad and Colleen started," he said.

I put a big bite of cake in my mouth, so I wouldn't have to say why.

Joey kept talking. "Grandpa told me you might be feeling a little scared now that we're going to be a family, and that maybe you're worried you might be left out of things. Is he right?"

I didn't really want to tell Joey that that was exactly how I've been feeling, but since Grandpa Winston said it and everybody knows old people are usually right, I nodded my head yes, and I told Joey that that's exactly how I've been feeling.

Then Joey surprised me. He said he

had something he wanted to tell me and
something he wanted to give me.

(I was hoping he would do the give-me
part first, but he didn't.)

Here's what he told me: He told me
that I wasn't the only one who is feeling
scared. He said that he's feeling scared
about some things too.

So I asked him what he's scared about,

and he told me. He said he's scared thinking about what it will be like when his dad and Mary Ann's mom get married and they all live in the same house.

He said he's not sure he'll like sharing his dad with Mary Ann and her mom. He said he can't imagine what it will be like having two more girls in his house. (I told him that part sounded like fun, but he said maybe not to him.)

Then, he said he's not sure what it will be like having a mom because he hasn't had one for a long time, and he doesn't know if he will like having Colleen as his.

And then he said something that really surprised me. He said that Winnie is scared too.

I asked him how he knew that, because one thing I knew for sure was that Winnie didn't tell him. But Joey said he knew because he heard Winnie talking to his grandpa, and he heard her say that she didn't want a new mother or a new sister, and that just thinking about what it will be like scares her.

And when he said that, it made me wonder. If Joey is scared and Winnie is scared, is Mary Ann scared too? Is she scared to move to Fern Falls? Does she feel afraid thinking about what it will be like to share her mom with Joey and Winnie? Is she nervous for Frank to be her dad?

Then I told Joey that I hadn't really thought about how all these changes would make anyone feel but me, but that I could see what he means about it all being scary for him too.

And then I told him if he ever wanted to talk about it with me, we could always have another heart-to-heart.

And that made Joey smile. Then he said he had something for me, but that first, he had a secret to tell me.

But I said, "No more secrets!"

So he said OK, and then he gave me something and guess what it was?

A giant chocolate Valentine's heart!!!!!!! (Mmmmm!)

And it had a little card attached to it. I couldn't wait to eat the heart, but I knew I had to read the card first.

Wait till you see what it said!

BEST BUDS

Mallory —
I hope you
like the candy.
Happy Valentine's
Day!
— Your secret
Admirer

LOVE

When I read the note, I couldn't believe
it. "Joey, I don't get it. You said you
weren't my secret admirer." I told him.

"I'm not," he said.

And that confused me. "Well if you're
not, who is?" I asked.

And that question made Joey laugh.

"That's the secret I was trying to tell you," Joey said. "It's not just me. It's me and my dad and my sister and my grandpa. We're all your secret admirers."

I guess Joey could tell I was confused because he kept explaining.

"Do you remember the day we went to the mall to get the skateboard for Mary Ann? Well, Dad thought it would be nice to get something for you too. And it was my idea to do it as your secret admirer. We all thought you might like that."

I almost fell off Joey's bed when he said that. I mean, it's one thing to have a secret admirer. It's a whole other thing to have a secret admiring family. "Wow!" I said.

"We're not the in-love-with-you type of secret admirer," he said. "We're more the friendly-cheerer-upper type."

And that made a lot of sense to me. The Winstons were just trying to make me feel better about everything that's going on. So I thanked Joey and told him that he and his family are very good

WORLD's BEST SECRET-ADMIRING FAMILY

friendly-cheerer-upper types of secret
admirers. Then I told him that I was
going to go thank the rest of his family.

But he said he had one more question
to ask me before I left. He asked me if
he could have a bite of my chocolate
heart. But I told him he'd have to get his
own chocolate heart. That this one was
from my secret admirer!

♡ *Mallory*

Girl Talk

STILL AT THE WISH POND

Dear Diary,

Do you remember that I told you I had 2 things to tell you? Well, here's thing #2:

Last night, when Mary Ann and I got home from the party, I told her I wanted to have a girl talk.

She said she was way too tired for any kind of talk, but I told her I would do most of the talking and she could do most of the listening. So we put on our matching heart pajamas, got into bed, and I started talking.

I told her about the heart-to-heart that Joey and I had and how he said that he and Winnie are both kind of scared about what things will be like once his dad and her mom get married.

I told her I was really surprised when Joey told me that because ever since Frank and Colleen started being Frank and Colleen, I thought I was the only one who had any reason to be scared.

Then I told Mary Ann that now that I know that Joey and Winnie are scared, it makes me wonder if she's feeling scared too, and that since I'm her best, best, best friend, she can tell me if she is.

Even though Mary Ann said she was too tired to talk, she told me that what she's feeling is mixed. She said she feels scared about some things and happy about others.

Here's what she said
she's scared about:

1. Her mom being
   married to someone
   other than her dad.
2. Being part of a new family.
3. Having Winnie as a stepsister (she
   said she's really scared about that,
   and I don't blame her).

Here's what she said she's
happy about:

1. Seeing her mom so happy.
2. Having Joey as a
   stepbrother.
3. Moving to Fern Falls and
   living next door to her lifelong best
   friend. (She means me, in case you
   weren't sure.) She said that's what
   she's the very happiest about.

Mary Ann told me that she talked about a lot of this stuff with her mom, who told her that it's normal to feel mixed, because with most things in life, there are parts that make you feel happy and other parts that might not.

And when she said that, I told Mary Ann that mixed is how I feel too. I told her that even though the idea of her and Joey becoming part of the same family and living in the same house makes me feel kind of left out, the idea of her being my next-door neighbor again really makes me excited.

And when I said that, Mary Ann said something to me I hadn't thought of before. "Just think," said Mary Ann. "When I move in next door, we can have pajama parties just like the ones we used to have and just like the one we're having now, all of the time."

And when she said that, I didn't feel mixed at all. I just felt happy. "Sleep tight and don't let the bedbugs bite," I said to Mary Ann.

And she said it right back, like she always does when we have pajama parties.

Then I told Cheeseburger goodnight, and I turned out the light.

A New Poem

Dear Diary,

I wrote a new poem for Frank and Colleen. I hope they'll be happy when they see it, and I hope they'll be happy together. At first, I wasn't too thrilled about them being a couple, but the truth is, I think they make a pretty good pair.

I thought you might like a sneak peek at the poem.

♡ Mallory

FRANK + COLLEEN = ♡ LOVE ♡

AWWWW!

Aren't they cute?

For Frank and Colleen

The Perfectest Pair
Frank and Colleen make THE perfectest pair!
Colleen loves Frank
   (though he's losing his hair).
Frank and Colleen make the perfectest pair!
Frank loves Colleen
   (like she's his teddy bear).
Frank and Colleen make the perfectest pair!
When they're not together,
   they're filled with despair.
Frank and Colleen make the perfectest pair!
Now that they're getting married,
   a life they will share.
Frank and Colleen make the perfectest pair!

  Big, huge hugs and kisses (I bet that's what you're going to give each other now),
   ♡ Mallory

Party Pics

Dear Diary,

When I gave Frank the new poem I wrote about Colleen and him, Frank gave me something too. Some pictures from the party. Here's one of Mom and Dad and Max and me. I think we look pretty good when we're all dressed up (even Max).

Here's a picture of the Winstons and Mary Ann and her mom. I still can't believe they're going to be one family now.

Frank even gave me pictures of me with Mary Ann and Joey. I guess there will be lots of pictures of the three of us together now that we're all going to be next-door neighbors.

When he gave these to me, he said that even though sometimes things change, and soon Mary Ann and Joey will be brother and sister, some things never change, and Mary Ann and Joey will always be my friends.

But when he said that, I told Frank that he was wrong.

I told him that Mary Ann and Joey are not my friends, they are my BEST friends. My BEST, BEST, BEST friends.

And as far as I'm concerned, that will never, ever change.

♡ *Mallory*

Valentines

Dear Diary,

One more thing. Valentines! I finally got in the mood and opened mine. Boy, am I glad I did. I got cards from everyone in my class and trust me when I tell you, they're cute, cute, cute.

But don't take my word for it. See a few for yourself.

To Mallory,
We hope you have a berry happy Valentine's Day.
Love, Arielle and Danielle

TO THE WORLD'S BEST VALENTINE
-Joey

To a student
who is all
Heart.
Love, Mrs.
Daily

See. Aren't they cute? I still do LOVE
Valentine's Day and this one turned out
to be great, even though I didn't think
there was any way that it would.

There's something else I LOVE, and
that is writing in you. I'm going to send

158

Grandma a great, big Valentine thank you card for giving you to me.

But guess what? I have to stop writing now. Mrs. Daily taught us the expression "That's all she wrote." She said it means that something is completely finished. And I am completely finished writing in you because I've used up all of the pages. No more room. BOO-HOO!

Thanks so, so, so much for being there when I needed you!

Big, huge hugs and kisses,
♡ Mallory

P.S. I would love to end my journal with a P.S., but I can't actually think of one.
P.P.S. I still can't think of one.
P.P.P.S. I'm still thinking.
P.P.P.P.S. I still can't think of one, but it doesn't matter anyway because I'm officially out of room...

Darby Creek
A division of Lerner Publishing Group, Inc.
241 First Avenue North
Minneapolis, MN 55401 U.S.A.

Website address: www.lernerbooks.com

Library of Congress Cataloging-in-Publication Data

Friedman, Laurie B.
     Heart to heart with Mallory / by Laurie Friedman ; illustrations by Barbara Pollak.
          p.   cm.
   Summary: Nine-year-old Mallory turns to her diary to sort through her emotions when she finds out she has a secret admirer and her two best friends' parents may be getting engaged.
     ISBN-13: 978-1-57505-932-7 (lib. bdg. : alk. paper)
     ISBN-10: 1-57505-932-0 (lib. bdg. : alk. paper)
   [1. Best friends—Fiction. 2. Friendship—Fiction. 3. Remarriage—Fiction. 4. Valentine's Day—Fiction. 5. Diaries—Fiction.] I. Pollak, Barbara, ill. II. Title.
   PZ7.F89773He 2006
   [Fic]—dc22   2005034106

Manufactured in the United States of America
8 — BP — 5/1/10